The Selfish Giant

Book by Kristin Walter
Music and Lyrics by Larisa Bryski

Based on a fairy tale by Oscar Wilde

Baker's Plays
7611 Sunset Blvd.
Los Angeles, CA 90042
BAKERSPLAYS.COM

THE SELFISH GIANT was originally produced on April 10, 2004 by Manhattan Children's Theatre. It was directed by Bruce Merrill with set design by Christie Phillips, costume design by Aaron Mastin, lighting design by Brian Byrne and music direction by Tim O'Brien. The cast included Jody Flader, Aaron Mize, Christina Pickard, Joseph Smith and Elliott Weinstock.

RENTAL MATERIALS

An orchestration consisting of **Piano/Vocal Scores** will be loaned two months prior to the production ONLY on the receipt of the Licensing Fee quoted for all performances, the rental fee and a refundable deposit.

Please contact Baker's Plays for perusal of the music materials as well as a performance license application.

CHARACTERS:

THE CHILDREN:

WINNIE, a mischievous young girl
BETH, a sweet young girl
MAX, a rambunctious young man
SARAH, a kind young girl

THE GIANT, a selfish old man

THE ELEMENTS:

SNOW, a glamorous female
FROST, a movie-star type male
NORTH WIND, a Rat-Pack type
HAIL, a dumb-blonde

Can also be done with 3f, 2m cast with the following doubling:

WINNIE/SNOW
MAX/FROST
BETH/NORTH WIND
SARAH/HAIL

SETTING

The action of the play takes place just outside and just inside the
Giant's garden, over the period of a year.

MUSICAL NUMBERS

In the Garden (**SARAH, WINNIE, BETH, MAX**)

The Giant's Song (**SARAH, GIANT**)

There's Music in the Air (**ALL**)

(Sound of school bell. Children's laughter is heard, turning into chattering as the children enter.)

WINNIE. What a beautiful day!

MAX. It is now.

BETH. Oh, school isn't that bad.

WINNIE. I love school.

MAX. I love it when the bell rings at the end of the day.

BETH. Oh, you just want to play all the time.

MAX. I sure do! You're it!

BETH. No fair! I wasn't ready. Come back here!

(Children play tag, laughing and arguing about the rules. They all collapse in a heap and sigh.)

WINNIE. What should we do now?

MAX. I don't know. What do you want to do?

BETH. I don't know. What do you want to do?

WINNIE. We could play hide and seek.

MAX. No, there aren't any good places to hide.

BETH. We could play statues!

MAX. We played statues yesterday.

BETH. We could play Follow the Leader!

MAX. I don't want to. I never get to be the leader.

WINNIE. Well, you think of something to do!

*(**SARAH** enters.)*

MAX. Look! There's the new girl!

BETH. We should invite her to play.

MAX. Why?

WINNIE. Because it's the nice thing to do.

MAX. But what if she's weird?

BETH. She's not weird.

MAX. You don't know that. You don't know anything about her. She could be from an alien planet, or maybe she's a robot.

WINNIE. Max! She's not a robot!

MAX. How do you know?

WINNIE. Because I know. Beth, do you know her name?

BETH. I think it's Sarah.

WINNIE. *(calling)* Sarah?

(She turns.)

Do you want to come and play with us?

SARAH. Sure. *(She comes over.)* Hi.

WINNIE. Hi.

BETH. Hi.

*(There's a pause. **BETH** hits **MAX**.)*

MAX. Hi.

WINNIE. I'm Winnie. This is Beth, and that's Max.

SARAH. I'm Sarah. It's nice to meet you.

BETH. So, where are you from?

MAX. Are you from Mars?

SARAH. *(laughs)* No. I used to live in the city. We just moved here last week.

WINNIE. Do you like it here?

SARAH. I guess so. I'm not really used to it yet.

MAX. Well, stick with us. We know how to have a good time!

SARAH. What are you doing?

MAX. We don't know. What do *you* want to do?

WINNIE. Oh, I have an idea! Let's go play in the garden!

BETH. The Giant's garden?

WINNIE. Of course.

MAX. Great idea, Winnie! Let's go!

SARAH. Wait! Did you say a giant?

WINNIE. Sure. He lives in that big house on the hill.

BETH. And he has a great garden.

MAX. It's huge! There's tons of space to run around.

WINNIE. He has the prettiest flowers in the whole village.

BETH. And the best peaches.

SARAH. He won't mind us playing there?

MAX. Oh, he's gone. No one has seen him for a long time.

BETH. He went away on a visit when we were small. I've never even seen him.

WINNIE. No one has ever seen him.

MAX. I saw him once.

BETH. You did not.

MAX. I did so. It was right before he left. He was coming out of the flower shop.

SARAH. What was he like?

MAX. He was ten feet tall. With three heads and green hair and long, pointy fangs.

SARAH. Really?

WINNIE. Max, stop it! You'll scare her.

SARAH. Are you sure he's gone?

MAX. He's gone. My father said he went to visit a friend.

BETH. I heard he was visiting an ogre.

MAX. Well, maybe the ogre *is* his friend.

WINNIE. There's nothing to be afraid of. I promise. We play in the garden all the time and nothing ever happens.

BETH. And it's so much fun in there!

MAX. There is plenty of room to play alien invasion. *(He starts to sneak around like an alien.)*

WINNIE. And there are so many hiding places.

MAX. The trees are perfect for climbing!

SARAH. The peaches do look good.

WINNIE. And the flowers are gorgeous!

SARAH. Well, if you're sure it's all right...

BETH. Of course it's all right. Let's go!

(They enter the garden.)

SARAH. Wow! This is great!

MAX. We told you. I'm going to climb that tree.

WINNIE. Can you get me a peach?

BETH. Sarah! Come here and smell these flowers.

SARAH. I can't believe how wonderful this is! We didn't have anything like this in the city.

MAX. Catch! *(He throws down some peaches.)*

WINNIE. Thanks, Max. So, Sarah, do you want to play tag, or statues or something?

SARAH. Can we just sit here for a minute?

BETH. What's the matter?

WINNIE. Are you okay?

SARAH. Oh, yes. It's just that…I had to leave all of my old friends back in the city, and I was so afraid that I would hate it here. And now I have all of you, and I'm in this beautiful garden…I'm just so happy.

WINNIE. The garden makes everyone happy.

SONG - In the Garden

SARAH.

> IT'S A BEAUTIFUL THING TO SEE
> THERE'S FRUIT ON EVERY TREE
> AND FLOWERS BLOOM AROUND US

WINNIE.

> IT'S A WONDERFUL KIND OF DAY
> IN SUCH A PLACE TO PLAY
> LET'S LEAVE OUR CARES BEHIND US

BETH.

> AND THE HAPPIEST GROUP OF BIRDS
> JUST WAITING TO BE HEARD
> SURROUND US WITH THEIR CHORUS

SARAH.

> ALL THE GREENERY IS SO TRUE,
> SO DAMP WITH EVENING DEW
> AS PURE AS ANY FOREST

MAX.

> OH, I LOVE THE FEEL OF GRASS BENEATH MY TOES,
> AND THE SCENT OF EVERY DAFFODIL AND ROSE,
> SO LONG AS THAT OLD GIANT STAYS AWAY FROM HERE-
> LET'S HOPE HE NEVER KNOWS!

ALL.

(CHORUS:)
IN THE GARDEN WE CAN LAUGH THE DAY AWAY,
AS WE CALL ON ALL OUR FRIENDS TO COME AND PLAY
AND WE'LL ALL KICK UP OUR HEELS, JUST TO KNOW HOW
GOOD IT FEELS
TO BE FREE…FREE TO STAY…IN THE GARDEN.

LET US GATHER ALL AROUND
TO MAKE A JOYFUL SOUND
AND SHARE THIS GIFT OF SPRINGTIME

'CAUSE WE KNOW THAT VERY SOON
WE'LL HAVE TO FACE THE MOON
WHEN DAY MAKES WAY FOR NIGHT TIME

BUT TOMORROW WE'LL COME BACK AGAIN, YOU'LL SEE
AND WE'LL EAT SOME PEACHES RIGHT OUT OF THAT TREE,
AND WE'LL SMELL THE FLOWERS ONCE AGAIN, AND LISTEN
TO THE
SOFTLY BLOWING BREEZE…

(CHORUS:)
IN THE GARDEN WE CAN LAUGH THE DAY AWAY,
AS WE CALL ON ALL OUR FRIENDS TO COME AND PLAY
AND WE'LL ALL KICK UP OUR HEELS, JUST TO KNOW HOW
GOOD IT FEELS
TO BE FREE…FREE TO STAY…IN THE GARDEN.

IN THE GARDEN.
IN THE GARDEN.
IN THE GARDEN.
IN THE GARDEN.

(From offstage, there is the sound of footsteps. The **CHIL-
DREN** *freeze and listen.)*

SARAH. Do you hear that?

MAX. Hear what?

WINNIE. It sounds like footsteps.

BETH. Big footsteps.

SARAH. Is it the Giant?

MAX. It can't be. He's gone.

BETH. Maybe he's back.

MAX. Well, maybe he won't mind us playing in the garden. He could be a nice giant.

(*The footsteps get louder and closer, until the* **GIANT** *appears with a roar.*)

GIANT. Who is in my garden? Children? Are there children in my garden?

WINNIE. We're sorry Mr…Giant…sir…

BETH. We didn't hurt anything.

SARAH. We were just playing.

GIANT. Did I give you permission to play in my garden? Get out! Get out, I tell you! This is my garden!

MAX. We didn't think you'd mind. After all, it's a big garden.

BETH. There's room for all of us.

WINNIE. You've done such a nice job with the flowers…

GIANT. This is my garden and my garden belongs to me. I planted those flowers and I watered those trees and I will allow no one to play here but myself. Now go!

WINNIE. We're going, sir.

SARAH. Please don't be angry.

GIANT. And don't come back!

BETH. We won't.

MAX. We promise.

(*The children run offstage.*)

GIANT. Children in my garden…Who said they could come into my garden? Look at this! It's a mess. Peach pits and trampled tulips, well, I'll have none of that. I will keep those children out, you just see if I can't. I'll…I'll build a fence. That'll keep those children out.

(*The* **GIANT** *begins to build a fence. The* **CHILDREN** *enter and watch this from the side, whispering to each other.*)

SARAH. I thought you said he was gone.

BETH. We thought he was.

WINNIE. I'm sorry, Sarah. He's been gone for such a long time – no one thought he'd ever come back.

MAX. It would have been better if he hadn't.

SARAH. What is he doing?

BETH. It looks like he's building a fence.

MAX. That's not fair!

BETH. It looks like it's going to be really high.

WINNIE. I can't even see the peach trees.

MAX. How are we supposed to get in there now?

BETH. We *won't* get in. That's the point.

WINNIE. He doesn't want us in.

MAX. But that's not fair!!

SARAH. Well, it *is* his garden. I guess he can build a fence and keep us out if he wants to.

WINNIE. Oh, Sarah. And you were feeling so happy.

BETH. We were having so much fun.

MAX. It's not fair!!!!!!!

(*The* GIANT *hangs a sign that says "Trespassers will be Prosecuted."*)

SARAH. What does that say?

BETH. Trespassers will be pros…prose…prosec…

WINNIE. Prosecuted.

MAX. What's prosecuted?

WINNIE. It means if we try to go into the garden, we'll get in trouble.

BETH. Will we get grounded?

WINNIE. Worse than that.

MAX. Worse than grounded?

WINNIE. I think it means we'll go to jail.

BETH. Jail!

MAX. We'd have to go to jail?! Just for going in the garden?

SARAH. But why? Why would the Giant build a fence to keep us out, and why would he prose…prose…prosecute us if we went in? We weren't hurting anything. He can't use that whole garden all by himself. There's enough for all of us.

WINNIE. I think he might be selfish.

MAX. I know he's selfish.

BETH. I guess he's just a selfish Giant.

(**CHILDREN** *exit.*)

GIANT. Now this is a fine fence. Strong and sturdy. I like fences. You always know where you stand with a fence. (*points*) My garden. Not my garden. See? Now there's no excuse for those children to be in my garden. I've got a fence *and* a sign. They can go off and find some other place to play. Like the street. And the village square. And come to think of it, they shouldn't be playing at all! They should be studying and working. Vagrants, that's what they are! Nothing but a pack of lazy vagrants. And they're not welcome in my garden!

(*The **GIANT** exits. The school bell rings. The **CHILDREN** enter. It is now autumn.*)

BETH. What do you want to play?

SARAH. I don't know. What do you want to play?

WINNIE. I don't know. What do you want to play, Max?

MAX. Nothing.

WINNIE. What's the matter?

MAX. We can't play in the square because we're too noisy. We can't play in the orchard because they're harvesting the apples, the creek's too high to cross so we can't play in the woods, and I'm tired of playing in the road.

BETH. It does get pretty dusty. My clothes have been a mess.

SARAH. And it's so full of those hard stones.

WINNIE. I've ripped two pairs of pants this month.

MAX. My knees hurt all the time. I hate it!

WINNIE. Oh, Max.

MAX. Well, I do! These were always the perfect days to play in the garden. We'd make piles of leaves and jump in them, we'd carve pumpkins from the pumpkin patch…

BETH. Remember picking all those apples?

WINNIE. We would make so much applesauce.

BETH. More than we could eat. We had to give most of it away.

WINNIE. Everyone in the village ate applesauce for weeks!

SARAH. It sounds wonderful!

MAX. I don't care about the old giant. I'm going back in the garden.

WINNIE. Max, don't!

BETH. You'll get in trouble!

MAX. He's a mean old giant.

(The **CHILDREN** *exit. Blackout. Sound of wind rushing)*

GIANT. Brrr. Such a biting wind – it chills me nearly to the bone. Winter is here. But the garden is ready. I gathered and burned the leaves – what a job that was, my hands are still blistered from the rake. I picked the apples and made them into sauce. It seems that there were more apples this year than I remembered. I had to throw half of them away. But the work is done, and I'm ready for winter. Lovely winter, with its snow and frost. The colder the better, that's what I say. Cold keeps the children inside and away from my garden.

(The **GIANT** *exits. Lights change. Wind continues to rush. We hear a tambourine, a triangle and chimes. The* **ELEMENTS** *enter, wearing masks that cover their faces. They play percussion instruments all through the scene as they decorate the garden with tinsel, cotton batting – anything that will make it look cold and wintery. They are very mysterious. **They should not be recognizable as the same actors who played the children.** They chant.)*

ELEMENTS.
Frost, cold, wind, snow
Never let the flowers grow.

Hail, sleet, rain, ice
Wintertime is rather nice.

HAIL.
Hailstones made from freezing rain
Bouncing off your windowpane.

SNOW.
> Snowy blankets ten feet deep
> Burying you while you sleep.

FROST.
> Freezing fingers, freezing toes
> Frostbite tickling your nose

NORTH WIND.
> Whipping wind that shrieks and moans
> Chilling you down to your bones.

ELEMENTS.
> Snow, frost, wind, hail
> Share with you this fairy tale.
> Now we'll end our little rhyme
> Welcome to the Wintertime!

> (**ELEMENTS** *exit. The sound of rushing wind gets louder. Lights come back to normal.* **WINNIE** *and* **SARAH** *enter, wearing winter coats.*)

SARAH. It gets colder here than it did in the city. Brrrr!

WINNIE. Where are your gloves?

SARAH. In my pocket.

WINNIE. Well, put them on. I'm putting on mine. *(She does.)*

> (**BETH** *and* **MAX** *run in.*)

MAX. Snowball fight!!!!! *(He throws a snowball at* **SARAH.***)*

SARAH. Hey! I'm cold enough already!

BETH. It's too bad they plowed the roads. There's hardly any snow left.

WINNIE. We can barely make a decent snowman.

SARAH. What are you talking about? There's tons of snow.

MAX. Yeah, but it's the dirty, slushy kind. We mean pure, untouched snow.

SARAH. Pure, untouched snow?

WINNIE. The kind that's powdery, but still sticky.

BETH. Perfect for snowmen.

MAX. And snowballs.

SARAH. Where do we find pure, untouched snow?

MAX. Where do you think?

SARAH. The garden?

BETH. The garden.

SARAH. It must have been so much fun to play there in the winter.

MAX. You have no idea. We used to divide up teams and make big forts and have huge snowball fights.

WINNIE. There were always a dozen snowmen around, with cute little carrot noses and corncob pipes.

BETH. Remember when Max made one that looked just like Mrs. Cameron?

SARAH. The school principal?

MAX. It was perfect! I gave her little wire frame glasses and a yardstick.

WINNIE. It was the funniest thing!

BETH. And then Mrs. Cameron saw it and we all thought Max was going to get in trouble…

SARAH. Was she mad?

MAX. Nope! She loved it so much she even knitted it a scarf and a little cap!

SARAH. It sounds so wonderful. I wish I could have been there.

WINNIE. I wish we could do it again this year.

MAX. Come on. I think there might be some good snow out behind my house. *(They exit.)*

*(The **GIANT** enters, carrying a snow shovel.)*

GIANT. There is so much snow to clear. Shoveling is such hard work, I almost wish my garden was a little bit smaller. I feel as though I've been shoveling for months. Every time I clear my garden, in comes another storm. And this has been a particularly bad winter. Last night I thought my roof would blow right off. Ah well, soon it will be spring. The warmth of the sun will bring out the grass and the flowers. Of course, it will also bring out those children. I've seen them peeking over the fence this winter. Good thing they can't get in. *(He shakes the fence.)* Strong and sturdy. Garden *in*…children *out.* The way it should be.

(The **GIANT** *exits.* **SNOW** *and* **FROST** *enter. They have a very languid, glamorous movie-star attitude about them. They are very cool, and they know it.)*

SNOW. Hello, Frost.

FROST. Hello, Snow. Having a good winter?

SNOW. One of the best. That extra cold snap last week was just what I needed. I feel great.

FROST. I hear that's the last snap of the season.

SNOW. Really? How dreadful. This has been such a nice season…I'm loathe to see it end.

FROST. There's no way around it. Spring is here.

SNOW. Green grass.

FROST. Warm breezes.

SPRING. Flowers.

FROST. Birdsong.

BOTH. *(shudder)* Ugh!

SNOW. It's just such a terrible bore.

FROST. Oh, I agree. Those mild temperatures; there's no passion, no extremes…

SNOW. And those colors…fuschia, violet, azure…

FROST. It's just so busy. At least pick one palette and go with that. I swear, if I see sunflowers anywhere near pink roses, I'll frost them so hard the petals break right off; I don't care what season it is.

SNOW. Well, look at that!

FROST. What?

SNOW. This garden. It looks like Little Miss Springtime missed a spot.

FROST. That's not like her. She's usually chomping at the bit by February.

SNOW. Well, let's take a look around…Excellent work on the flower beds, Frost.

FROST. Thank you. And the snow here – so smooth and even.

SNOW. Oooh, that *is* good work. Yay, me!

FROST. Wait! Do you hear that?

SNOW. I don't hear anything.

FROST. Exactly. No chattering, no giggling, no running about…

SNOW. No children! So that's why we have no spring fling.

FROST. She always was a sucker for the children.

SNOW. Well, even I'll admit enjoying their little antics, but Spring…she *needs* them.

FROST. But it's not like her to just ignore a garden – even one without children. There has to be more to it than that.

SNOW. Well, let's see. We have flower beds, and peach trees and I saw a pumpkin patch around the back.

FROST. And there's this fence.

SNOW. Oooh, it's so strong and sturdy. Built to keep something inside.

FROST. *(sees the sign)* Or something out. Take a look at this.

SNOW. "Trespassers will be prosecuted." Well, now it all makes sense. Spring isn't going to hang around where she isn't wanted. I wonder who owns this garden.

FROST. Shhh! I hear someone coming.

*(The **GIANT** enters.)*

GIANT. There seems to be a new storm brewing. It's odd; I thought Spring was on its way. I'll just check to see if my fence will hold up. *(He checks the fence.)* Good. That will keep the children from eating my peaches and picking my flowers. They can just stay away. This is MY garden!

(He exits.)

FROST. What a horrible man!

SNOW. He's so dreadfully mean.

FROST. And so selfish.

SNOW. It's no wonder Spring passed him by.

FROST. She'll never want to come here again.

SNOW. Just think – a garden forever in Winter.

FROST. Bitterly cold.

SNOW. With icy winds.

FROST. Gray clouds.

SNOW. Hail!

FROST. Snow!

SNOW. Frost!

SNOW & FROST. I love it!!!!

FROST. Good bye, springtime!

SNOW. We can stay here all year round.

FROST. Summer will leave us alone.

SNOW. Autumn won't bother to come here either.

FROST. Get comfy, darling. We're moving in!

SNOW. Oooh! Let's give Hail and North Wind a jingle. They'd love this place! *(She rings a set of sleigh bells.)*

> *(***NORTH WIND*** *and* **HAIL** *enter.* **NORTH WIND** *is very Rat Pack, while* **HAIL** *is the typical Hollywood blonde.)*

NORTH WIND. *(singing)* I hear those sleigh bells jingling, ring ting tingling, too. You rang?

HAIL. Hi there, girls. What's going on?

FROST. Hello Hail. How're you doing, North Wind?

NORTH WIND. Can't complain. What's new with you?

FROST. We thought you might like to join our little party.

HAIL. A party! I love parties!

SNOW. What do you think of our new garden?

> *(***NORTH WIND*** *and* **HAIL** *walk around the garden.)*

NORTH WIND. Something's not right here.

SNOW. Really?

NORTH WIND. Definitely something amiss.

FROST. Whatever can it be?

NORTH WIND. I can't quite put my finger on it.

HAIL. Why is it so cold in here?

NORTH WIND. That's it! It's still winter!

SNOW. Isn't it fabulous?

NORTH WIND. Check out all the snow!

SNOW. Thank you; I'm proud of it.

NORTH WIND. And that frost – that's museum quality.

FROST. It's an art.

HAIL. I don't understand. Why is it winter here, but it's spring over there?

NORTH WIND. Did little "pocket full of posies" Spring forget to drop by?

SNOW. Look at the sign.

HAIL. "Trespassers will be pros… prose…"

FROST. Prosecuted.

HAIL. What's prosecuted?

SNOW. It means that anyone who tries to come into this garden will be thrown in jail.

HAIL. What kind of a mean man would put up a sign like that?

NORTH WIND. My kind of mean man!

SNOW. As long as Spring isn't kicking up her heels we can chill out in here as long as we want.

FROST. I'm cool. What about you, North Wind? Feel like sticking around?

NORTH WIND. I was headed up to the Arctic, but I can blow that off. What d'ya say, Hail?

HAIL. *(oblivious to the conversation)* What?

SNOW. Ooooh, she's giving you the cold shoulder.

NORTH WIND. *(buttering her up)* My little Hailstone, little popsicle, my sweet little Eskimo Pie – you wanna live here for a while?

HAIL. Hooray! It'll be like, Winter forever!

SNOW. I want that spot by the pumpkin patch! It's perfect for making moguls!

FROST. I'm headed for the windows of the house. If you need me, I'll be making gorgeous patterns!

NORTH WIND. There are some loose shingles on the roof. They won't be there for long.

HAIL. Look at the shed! It has a tin roof! I looooove tin roofs! They make the best noises. It's like…music.

ELEMENTS.
> FROST, COLD, WIND, SNOW
> NEVER LET THE FLOWERS GROW.
> HAIL, SLEET, RAIN, ICE
> WINTERTIME IS RATHER NICE.
> SNOW, FROST, WIND, HAIL
> SHARE WITH YOU THIS FAIRY TALE.
> NOW WE'LL END OUR LITTLE RHYME
> IT'S FOREVER WINTERTIME!

(The **ELEMENTS** *exit. The* **GIANT** *enters. It is now the end of the summer.)*

GIANT. I don't understand. Spring came and went in the village. Every tree blossomed, the grass was green, the flowers grew. It turned to summer, the peaches came out on the trees; the sun was warm. Except in my garden. Spring came, but not to my garden. Summer came, but not to my garden. Autumn is here, but not in my garden. I don't understand.

*(***GIANT*** exits.* **CHILDREN** *enter.)*

WINNIE. The summer went by so fast.

MAX. Too fast. I can't believe we have to go back to school already.

BETH. I'm looking forward to going back to school. A new classroom, a new teacher…

MAX. New homework…

WINNIE. You can't fool us, Max. We know you really like school.

MAX. That information is classified. I'll never tell. You'd have to torture me first!

BETH. That doesn't sound like a bad idea. *(She starts to tickle him.)*

WINNIE. *(notices* **SARAH** *looking at the garden, which is still covered with snow)* What is it, Sarah?

SARAH. I'm just looking at the garden. I can't believe it's still winter in there. It's so weird.

MAX. How many times do I have to tell you, the garden is a site for secret government experiments. It's covered in an invisible force field and they're bombarding it with gamma rays.

BETH. Gamma rays?

MAX. Well, something radioactive. It's like…a nuclear winter.

WINNIE. No one knows what's going on.

MAX. I'm telling you, it's toxic. I think I'm growing a third eye.

SARAH. Max, quiet!

MAX. Whoa. What's the matter with you?

SARAH. I don't know. I just keep thinking that the Giant is all alone in there.

BETH. It's his own fault. He built the fence and put up the sign. He seems to want to be left alone.

SARAH. Maybe. But I feel sorry for him. We all have each other, but he doesn't have anyone at all.

WINNIE. He has the garden. Sort of.

SARAH. I guess.

MAX. Come on, let's get out of here. *(***BETH*** is staring at him.)* What?

BETH. Oh my gosh! You really *are* growing a third eye!!

MAX. *(grabbing his forehead)* Where?!

BETH. Gotcha!

(She runs offstage, chased by **MAX** *and followed by* **WINNIE** *and* **SARAH.** *The* **GIANT** *enters. It is now spring again, and still winter in the garden.)*

GIANT. A year. It has been winter in my garden for a full year. Why? I want to know why! It's only a fence

– boards and nails – *(shakes the fence)* How can this make the world stand still? *(He hears birdsong and sees a bird on the other side of the fence.)* A bird! Oh, please, little bird, will you come into my garden? Will you sing for me? Please, don't go! *(He drops to his knees.)* The flowers! *(He starts to dig through the snow.)* Where are they? I planted flowers! Grow! Grow, please!… why won't you grow? Why?

SONG - THE GIANT'S SONG

AS I LOOK OVER THE FENCE
I CAN SEE THAT IN THE WEST THE SUN IS GLOWING
BUT BITTER IS THE COLD
THAT LIVES INSIDE THESE WALLS – IT NEVER SEEMS TO END.

AND SO I STAND HERE ALL ALONE
WITH SADNESS IN MY HEART AS IT KEEPS SNOWING
OH, HOW I WISH THAT I COULD
FIND A LAUGH TO MEND MY BROKEN HEART AGAIN.

PLEASE HELP ME UNDERSTAND THIS
I WANT TO FIND A REASON
I WISH THAT SPRING WOULD COME BACK
AND CHASE WINTER AWAY.
JUST A FEW BRIGHT FLOWERS
SOME SMALL SIGNS OF THE SEASON
A BLUEBIRD ON MY WINDOWSILL
AND CHILDREN HERE TO PLAY

SARAH.

I TRY TO STAY AWAY BUT STILL
THE BEAUTY OF THE GARDEN CALLS OUT TO ME.
THE HAPPINESS I FELT THERE WARMED MY HEART
AND MADE ME FEEL PART OF A WHOLE.

MAYBE IF I CLIMB THE FENCE
AND LET THE SPRINGTIME WORK ITS MAGIC THROUGH ME
I COULD TEACH THE GIANT HOW IT FEELS
TO LOVE WITH ALL HIS HEART AND ALL HIS SOUL.

SARAH & GIANT.

PLEASE HELP ME UNDERSTAND THIS

I WANT TO FIND A REASON
I WISH THAT SPRING WOULD COME BACK
AND CHASE WINTER AWAY.
JUST A FEW BRIGHT FLOWERS
SOME SMALL SIGNS OF THE SEASON
A BLUEBIRD ON MY WINDOWSILL
AND CHILDREN HERE TO PLAY.

A BLUEBIRD ON MY WINDOWSILL
AND CHILDREN HERE TO PLAY.

(**GIANT** *exits.*)

SARAH. This isn't right. I don't care if he is selfish and mean, he needs help. And if no one else will help him, I will. I have to… (*She starts to climb the fence. The other* **CHILDREN** *enter.*)

WINNIE. Sarah, stop!

BETH. You can't!

MAX. You'll get electrocuted by the force field!

SARAH. I don't care! The Giant is in there somewhere, and he's lonely and he needs us!

BETH. He'll just throw us out again.

MAX. Or use us for his experiments.

SARAH. No, he won't.

WINNIE. How do you know?

SARAH. I just *know.* I can't explain it, but I do. We can bring the springtime back to the garden. All we have to do is go in. Are you with me?

BETH. I'm in. It's crazy, but I'm in.

WINNIE. Are you sure about this?

SARAH. I've never been more sure of anything in my life.

WINNIE. Then I'm in.

SARAH. Max?

MAX. You have to ask? Of course I'm in!

SARAH. Then let's go.

(*They climb the fence and enter the garden.*)

BETH. It's freezing in here!

MAX. What now?

SARAH. I'm not sure. *(She walks around.)* Wait! It's getting warmer.

WINNIE. She's right.

BETH. This is crazy!

SARAH. I'm going to touch the flower beds.

WINNIE. Be careful!

MAX. I can't watch!

  *(**SARAH** touches the flower bed. The snow disappears.)*

BETH. Did you see that?

MAX. Move over, Sarah, I'm giving this a try. *(He touches another flower bed. The snow disappears.)* Wow!

  *(The **CHILDREN** grow excited. Laughing, they run around the garden, making the snow disappear and shouting: "It's warming up!" "The grass is growing!" "I see flowers!" etc. The **GIANT** enters.)*

GIANT. I thought I heard a bird singing. I was in my room and I heard it… *(He sees the children and that spring has come into the garden.)* It's spring. It's spring! There are flowers and birds and sunshine, and there are children in my garden!

WINNIE. We're sorry, sir.

SARAH. Are you angry?

MAX. Don't vaporize us with your ray gun!!

BETH. We'll leave if you want us to.

GIANT. No! No, please don't go! It is your doing that there is spring in my garden. Your laughter brought it back. Thank you, children, thank you! I was selfish; I wanted the garden all for myself, but without all of you, it was no garden at all. Can you ever forgive me?

WINNIE. Of course we can.

BETH. We're just so happy to be back in the garden.

MAX. Mr. Giant, sir?

GIANT. Yes?

MAX. Can we take the sign down? I really don't want to go to jail. My parents would kill me.

GIANT. We can do better than that, young man. Let's take down the whole fence!

MAX. Really?

WINNIE. That's wonderful!

BETH. Wait until the kids at school hear about this!

(The children start to take the fence down. The **GIANT** *stops* **SARAH**.*)*

GIANT. How did you know? How did you know that you could melt the snow?

SARAH. There's magic in this garden. I felt it the first time I came here. It was so beautiful – it made me feel welcome. It made me feel at home.

GIANT. You will always be at home here. *(to everyone)* Tell your friends! Tell the whole village! This is OUR garden!

SONG - THERE'S MAGIC IN THE AIR

ALL:

LOOK AT WHAT HAS BEEN CREATED –
MORE THAN JUST A NEW BEGINNING
SPRING IS HERE AND WINTER'S GONE AWAY

AS WE STAND HERE ALL TOGETHER
SHARING ALL THIS GARDEN BEAUTY
FRIENDSHIP BLOOMS IN THE LIGHT OF A NEW DAY

AND NOW, NO ONE'S LONELY ANYMORE
THERE'S PLENTY OF ROOM FOR EVERYONE
THERE'S LAUGHTER AND HAPPINESS AGAIN
AND MAGIC IN THE AIR AROUND US ALL
      (MAGIC IN THE AIR AROUND US ALL...)

NOW IT'S TIME FOR CELEBRATING
DANCE AND SING AND SMELL THE FLOWERS
WATCH THE CLOUDS MAKE SHAPES ACROSS THE SKY

EVERY BLADE OF GRASS IS SPECIAL
EVERY LEAF AND EVERY PETAL
WE ARE TOO; WE DON'T EVEN HAVE TO TRY

AND SO, AS WE BID OUR FRIENDS FAREWELL
THERE'S PLENTY OF LOVE FOR EVERYONE
THERE'S LAUGHTER AND HAPPINESS AGAIN
AND MAGIC IN THE AIR AROUND US ALL
      (MAGIC IN THE AIR AROUND US ALL…)

(8 bar interlude)

LOOK AT WHAT HAS BEEN CREATED –
MORE THAN JUST A NEW BEGINNING
SPRING IS HERE AND WINTER'S GONE AWAY

AS WE STAND HERE ALL TOGETHER
SHARING ALL THIS GARDEN GLORY
FRIENDSHIP BLOOMS IN THE LIGHT OF A NEW DAY

AND NOW, NO ONE'S LONELY ANYMORE
THERE'S PLENTY OF ROOM FOR EVERYONE
THERE'S LAUGHTER AND HAPPINESS AGAIN
THERE'S MAGIC IN THE AIR
WE DON'T EVEN HAVE TO TRY
'CAUSE WINTER'S GONE AWAY
YES, THERE'S MAGIC IN THE AIR AROUND US ALL.

The End

Also by
Kristin Walter...

The Elves and the Shoemaker

Hansel & Gretel

Last of the Dragons

Rapunzel

OTHER TITLES AVAILABLE FROM BAKER'S PLAYS

THE ELVES AND THE SHOEMAKER

Kristin Walter

Comedy / 3f, 2m / multiple settings

Unfortunately, Eric, the lone shoemaker of Grimmsville, makes shoes that are miserably uncomfortable and impossible to walk in...leaving a lot of barefoot villagers and Eric without a means to provide for his family. While his wife tries to be supportive, his daughter Shannon just can't take it anymore! Sitting alone in the woods pondering her family's fate, Shannon is confronted by a stranger who offers her the deal of a lifetime... in exchange for her torturous pair of shoes, she is given a magical medallion that holds "the charm of the elves." Wanting to help her family, Shannon tries the chant. Her words beckon a pair of elves that show up night after night at the shoemaker's home creating the most fabulous shoes EVER! With his shoes now wanted throughout the land, Eric and his family have more gold than they can count. But they quickly begin to realize that all the money in the world doesn't necessarily buy happiness.

"...the script by Kristin Walter is a joy - true to the original story, but with enough clever asides to keep the parents in the audience laughing along with the kids."
- nytheatre.com

"Walter is a clever playwright. She masterfully writes one line for the children to enjoy and follows it up with a quick-witted one that seems to nudge the parent in the rib."
- Off-Off Broadway Review